D0612264

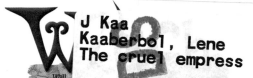

Printed in the United States of America
First U.S. edition
1 3 5 7 9 10 8 6 4 2

This book is set in 11.5/16 Hiroshige Book.
ISBN 0-7868-0979-5
Visit www.clubwitch.com

Will Irma Taranee Cornelia Hay Lin

ADVENTURES

The Cruel Empress

By Lene Kaaberbol

an imprint of
HYPERION BOOKS FOR CHILDREN
New York

Once, long ago, when the universe was young, spirits and creatures lived under the same sky. There was only one world, only one vast realm, governed by the harmonies of nature. But evil entered the world, and found its place in the hearts and minds of spirits and creatures alike, and the world shattered into many fragments. The realm was split between those who wished for peace and those who lived to gain power over others and cause them pain. To guard and protect what was good in the worlds, the mighty stronghold of Candracar was raised in the middle of infinity.

There, a congregation of powerful spirits and creatures keep vigilance; chief among them is the Oracle. His wisdom is much needed; at times,

Candracar is all that keeps evil from entering where it should have no place.

There is also the Veil. A precious barrier between good and evil, guarded by unlikely girls.

Irma has power over water. Taranee can control fire. Cornelia has all the powers of earth. Hay Lin holds the lightness and the freedom of air. And Will, the Keeper of the Heart of Candracar, holds a powerful amulet in which all of the natural elements meet to become energy, pure and strong.

Together they are W.I.T.C.H.—five Guardians of the Veil. And the universe needs them. . . .

1

"Up," said my father. "Why won't you just get up?"

He was standing on Park Hill, talking—actually, it was more like arguing—with a kite. The dragon-shaped kite jerked and sagged, giving the impression that it had no intention of taking flight. My father wiggled his fingers and worked the kite lines skillfully, but it was a lost cause.

Trying not to catch my father's attention, I turned my back and whispered a few kind words to the wind. All at once, the huge kite rose and soared into the sky. I looked up and smiled. Red and yellow ribbons flickered like flames from the dragon's mouth. The kite dipped and played in the currents of air.

"There," cried my dad. "Now she's flying."

I walked over to him and linked my arm with

his, careful not to disturb the kite lines. Everything was peaceful, and I let out a sigh. "It looks beautiful," I said.

"It certainly does," said Dad, with a smile of satisfaction. My father had every right to be satisfied. After all, the kite was a present that I had made especially for him.

I have always loved making things and being creative. Some people say that I am free-spirited and artsy. If that means that I love painting and funky outfits, then that's me! I just like the feeling of creating my own style—and, of course, having others notice my creations. Once, I even had my own fashion show! The show was held at school, and the local paper did a whole article about it. All my friends helped out with the modeling and lighting and stuff. It was a great feeling when everyone stood up and applauded for my clothes. I felt like I was in a movie—especially when we had to go on a mission right afterward to save a world from a giant worm.

My other great passion is painting. That is why, for my father's birthday, I decided to try to paint something new and extra special—a kite. I wanted it to be the most beautiful kite my dad had ever owned. He loves kites, and every spring he gets a new one that he spends the rest of the year flying until it is all battered and torn. I was determined to use all of my creative juices to make him a fabulous one.

Unfortunately, while I can make cool clothes for my friends or create a handbag to give as a gift, I had no clue how to make a kite. But I wasn't about to let that stop me. At the crafts store, I found patterns and fabrics and then spent ages sewing the various pieces together. I used all of my dad's favorite colors and painted a large silver dragon's face on the kite. Then I added the ribbons, to make it look as though the dragon were breathing fire. After all, our family restaurant is the Silver Dragon, so I thought the kite design was perfect for my dad.

It took a lot longer than I thought it would to make a kite. My friends thought it was funny that I would rush home after school to sew or paint, but it was worth the effort. When he opened his present, my dad was speechless. He just looked at the kite, then at me, and then back at the kite. It was as if he couldn't believe that his little Hay Lin had made the object that he held in his hands. It was the best feeling in the world.

But now, as I watched my dad negotiate the strings of the kite, I couldn't help feeling a little sad. I let out a big sigh. Last year, my grandma had been there to fly kites with us. Now, that seemed long ago. She would have loved the kite. It felt strange to think that she would never see it.

My father heard my sigh and turned his attention away from the kite toward me.

"What's wrong, Hay Lin?" he asked.

"Nothing," I said, trying to sound cheerful. It was a beautiful, breezy, spring Saturday, and my dad had finally snagged a few hours away from the restaurant. I didn't want to spoil it for him by being such a downer. But he knew me too well.

"Are you thinking about Grandma?" he asked.

"I guess I just really miss her," I admitted. "Remember how much she used to love flying kites? I wish she could be here now."

At my grandmother's funeral, the sadness had been overwhelming. I felt as if she had abandoned us, and I wasn't sure how my family would manage without her. Of course, I later found out that my grandmother hadn't really left me. In reality, she was a Guardian and had gone to live with the Oracle in Candracar. But that didn't make it any easier or mean I missed her any less.

"I miss her, too," my dad said after a moment. "But we should remember her and cherish all the wonderful things she said and did, even as we go on with our lives. It's the only thing to do. And don't you think she would want us to enjoy your beautiful kite, Hay Lin?"

I couldn't help smiling. I knew my dad was right. Once again, I felt myself relax.

Just at that moment, I heard the sound of someone calling our names. It was my mother, and she sounded upset.

"What's wrong?" asked my father as he walked down the hill.

"It's Uncle Kao," she said. "He fell. . . . They've taken him to the hospital, and the doctor thinks we should come."

My father's hands jerked, and the dragon crashed to the ground in one swoop.

"What's wrong with him?" I asked.

My mother hesitated. "We'll have to see," was all she said.

Uncle Kao looked small and pale against the white hospital sheets. I knew he was old; but he usually didn't look this tired.

"Hello, Hay Lin," he said to me, but although he smiled, his voice was weak.

"Hi, Uncle Kao," I said. We all call him Uncle, even though he isn't really our uncle. He's an old friend of my grandmother's, and a sort of honorary godfather to all of us. For as long as I can remember, he's always been around.

Outside, in the brightly lit hallway, I could hear my father and Uncle Kao's granddaughter, my cousin Lee, talking. But in my uncle's room, the lights were dim and soft.

"It was nice of you to come see a clumsy old man," Uncle Kao said. "At my age, you'd think I would have figured out how to walk without falling down," he added with a chuckle.

I didn't know what to say. It felt weird to hear him joking around. After all, he was in a hospital! I took his hand and held it tightly in mine.

"It's not the fall that's the issue," I heard cousin Lee tell my father, out in the hall. "Now they say he has pneumonia."

"But aren't there antibiotics?" asked my father. "People don't die of pneumonia these days!"

Through the glass window in Uncle Kao's room, I saw cousin Lee put a reassuring hand on my dad's shoulder. "Of course they don't," she said. "I'm sure he'll be just fine."

Uncle Kao sighed, and I knew he had heard the discussion through the doorway, too. And that he had also heard the note of doubt in cousin Lee's voice.

He looked exhausted.

"Maybe we should leave," I said. "You probably need to rest." I got up to go.

"Not yet!" Uncle Kao said. His hand closed around mine. "There's something . . . something I have to say to you. Something you have to have. Your grandmother left it in my keeping many years ago. She told me you were to have it when the time was right. I'm not sure whether this is the right time or not, but for me it could be the only time. So you tell my granddaughter to give you Liu's lantern."

He closed his eyes, and his breathing grew quieter. For a moment, I thought he might have fallen asleep. As I started to leave, Uncle Kao opened his eyes and looked at me once more.

"Don't forget—Liu's lantern," he said.

"I won't. I promise, Uncle Kao," I said before turning once more to leave.

"Good," he replied. Then he muttered under his breath, "Maybe now she'll quit bugging me!"

I was pretty sure that the "she" he was talking about was my grandmother.

I should have guessed that this was going to be another adventure for me and my friends.

When you're a Guardian of the Veil, nothing is simple. Even a message from your grandmother!

2

Since I had promised Uncle Kao that I would see about the lantern he had been mumbling about, I called my cousin first thing the next morning. When I told her what I needed, she agreed to drop the mysterious lantern off on her way back from the hospital. But, by the time she finally arrived at the restaurant, I was getting pretty anxious. I'm not good at waiting. She handed me a box and updated my family on Uncle Kao's condition.

After the rest of the family wandered off, Lee stayed for a moment. I opened the box. Inside was a small, delicate lantern with a lacquered black frame, thin and yellowed rice-paper sides, and, hanging down from the frame, four fading red-silk tassels. It was like nothing I'd ever seen before.

"It's beautiful," I said. Then I looked up at Lee. I had one question I *needed* to ask before she left. "Do you know who Liu is?"

"I'm not really sure," Lee said. "Your grandmother always called this Liu's lantern, but no, I never knew who Liu was."

I thought about what Uncle Kao had said the night before. He mentioned that I was supposed to have the lantern "when the time was right." But that didn't make any sense. If my grandmother had wanted me to have it, why wouldn't she have given the lantern to me herself? Why leave it for Uncle Kao to do?

I sat staring at the lantern for a long time after Lee left. For some reason I couldn't take my eyes off it. In some weird way, I felt drawn to the thing.

Without even thinking, I began to sketch the lantern. It was hard, because there was so much detail, but I didn't mind. It was kind of nice to get lost in drawing. I could forget the sadness of the past few days. Focusing on the sketch pad, I tried to get the tassels just right and make the rice paper seem as fragile as it looked. I was so busy sketching away that I was suprised when my mother called me down to dinner. I hadn't even realized that it was already dark out. Stuffing the picture in my pocket, I went downstairs to eat.

I had many questions for Uncle Kao. So I was antsy all through dinner, trying to rush my parents along with the meal so we could go and visit Uncle Kao.

"What is your hurry?" my mother asked as I jumped up to clear the table.

It turned out that we were too late. Uncle Kao was asleep by the time we arrived at the hospital. I didn't think finding out Liu's identity was a good enough reason to wake him. Looking at Uncle Kao lying helplessly in the hospital bed, I felt another wave of sadness. Reaching into my pocket, I pulled out the sketch of the lantern and put the drawing on his bedside table. At least that way, when he woke up, he would know that I had followed his instructions.

Later that night, in my room, I stared at the lantern. I started to blame it for what had happened. I would not have the lantern if Uncle Kao hadn't fallen, I thought. But still, there was something about it, a fragile beauty, that melted my bitterness. I went downstairs and asked my mom for a candle.

"Now?" she said, putting away the last load of dishes from the restaurant. "What do you want a candle for? You have school tomorrow; you should be in bed."

"I was going to light my lantern," I said softly. "I thought it would be nice to fall asleep to."

She stopped what she was doing for a minute and pushed her hair away from her forehead. "Are you okay, Hay Lin?" she asked gently.

"I'm fine," I said. "It's just . . . I just wish Uncle Kao was better."

"I know, sweetie. So do I," she whispered. "We *all* want him to feel better."

She hugged me briefly, then tilted my face and looked straight into my eyes.

"Do you know what your grandmother used to tell me?" she said. "Whenever I was feeling down, she would say, 'It is better to light a small candle than to sit around complaining about the dark.' I always thought that was a very wise saying. Go on and light your candle. But be careful—that lantern is very old."

"I'll be careful," I said. "I just thought it looked wrong without a candle. It's meant to be lit up inside."

Again my mother gave me a concerned look. The she leaned forward and rested her hand against my cheek for a moment. Her fingers were hot and damp from washing the dishes.

"You're a lot like your grandmother," she said with a smile.

I went back upstairs to my room and lit the lantern.

In the soft glow it cast, I could see that there was a delicate pattern on the rice-paper panels that I had missed in my earlier sketch. There was also a depiction of a large, smiling sun, and mountains surrounded by trees. The light and the smell of the burning candle was comforting, and I found myself thinking about Grandma. I wondered if she knew I had been given the lantern, and that I liked it.

Carefully, I blew out the candle and crawled into bed. I could still smell the candle smoke as I drifted off to sleep. The mountain image from the lantern must have followed me into my dreams, because that night I dreamed of the mountains and the trees. In the dream there was a girl calling my name, and the gentle sound of wind chimes.

The next morning I heard wind chimes again, as I rode my bike to school. But these chimes were the real thing—a set of slim silver rods twinkled in the early morning sun outside the entrance to a small shop. A slight breeze was making the rods knock and dance against each other, creating a delicate, tinkling music.

I stopped my bike. I felt drawn to the chimes by the strongest feeling, as if someone had had a kite line tied to my middle, and were reeling me in. I was powerless to resist the sensation.

I had seen the store many times before. I passed it every day on my way to school. It was called the China Shop. But I had never been inside it. Even though there were paintings and sculptures inside that looked interesting, I had never thought to stop in.

Today, though, something felt different. I got off my bike and walked up to the door. I had to see what was inside. I just had to. I opened the door and went in.

The store was dimly lit and full of shadows. After being out in the morning sunlight, I felt almost blinded. Slowly, I moved further into the dark recesses of the shop, where I noticed a bright light.

The spot of light came from an old mirror in a metal frame. The glass was so clouded with age and dirt that I could barely see myself, and yet I couldn't stop staring at it.

"Welcome to the China Shop," said a soft voice behind me. "May I help you?"

I whirled around.

A young woman had emerged from the back

room. She looked perfectly normal and ordinary, dressed in jeans and a sweater, but there was something about her eyes . . . something familiar.

"This mirror . . ." I began, and then I hesitated, not knowing what I wanted to say. Did I want to buy the mirror? Yes! I did! Suddenly, I had to have it—it was completely necessary. "How much is it?" I finally asked, my voice squeaking with excitement.

"It's not too expensive. But it's very old—we have new ones that are much nicer," the woman said, smiling kindly.

"No," I said quickly. "This one is fine."

Just then it occurred to me that I didn't have any money on me. Not even enough to buy an old, not-too-expensive mirror. "I guess I'll have to come back later. I don't have any money to pay you right now," I explained. I tried to sound sincere. I didn't want the woman to think I was trying to cheat her. "But could you please not sell it to anyone else until I get back?"

"Why don't you take it now?" she said sweetly. "You can always come back and pay me later."

I was surprised. It made me kind of nervous that this woman was being so nice. Why was she letting me take the mirror before paying for it?

"How do you know that I'll come back with money?" I asked. "I could just take the mirror and never come back."

"You're not the kind of person who would do that," she said, with what seemed like complete confidence. "You keep your promises, and you do what is required. Am I right?"

"I usually keep my promises," I said. Yes, I do, I repeated to myself. But . . . how did she know that? I had never met this woman before, and she knew way too much about me.

It didn't seem to matter, because she had already taken the mirror off its hook and was wrapping it in newspaper.

"Good. That is important." She passed me the package. "And now, shouldn't you get going? You must have school."

School! I had totally forgotten. I was going to be so late. I slipped the package gently into my bag and walked toward the doorway. As I opened the door, the chimes tinkled softly, reminding me of my dream. I hesitated.

"These chimes . . ." I began to say.

"You don't need the chimes," the woman said before I could finish. "Just the mirror. Farewell, Little One."

I stared at her. Had I heard her right? This was

weird. How did this stranger know my family nickname, the name that my grandmother had used to call me? For a moment it seemed to me that the eyes that looked back at me from that young face were my grandmother's.

My head was full of questions. But the woman held up her hand.

"Go now," she said. "I'll see you later." And once again, she looked perfectly ordinary and ungrandmotherly.

I shook my head, not knowing what to think. But I didn't have time to think; I was late for school. I got on my bike and raced down the street.

But there was even more strangeness to come that morning.

It turned out that I wasn't late for school after all. Well, I was a little late, but only half a minute or so. It was as if what had happened in the China Shop had taken no time at all.

3

"That's really weird," said Irma, when I told her and the others while we were eating lunch later that day about what had happened. Great! Typical Irma response, I thought—lighthearted but not too helpful.

"Do you think there was magic involved?" I asked in a whisper. Surrounded by the everyday school life of classes, gossip, quizzes, and the like, the oddness of my morning's encounter had faded into the background. I was beginning to think it could have just been my imagination. I began idly to sketch Liu's lantern in a notepad. I had been doing that all day. My notebooks were now covered with pictures of the lantern and images of my grandmother. I knew the two things were connected; I just couldn't figure out how.

"Sounds like something W.I.T.C.H. should

look into," said Irma, her blue eyes growing serious. "I think you should go back to that shop, and I'm definitely coming with you. I want to see this for myself."

"I think I'll come, too," Will chimed in, turning to look directly at me. "Hey, you with us, Hay Lin? Up for another store visit? I don't want to interrupt your drawing," she added, smiling.

Looking up from my notebook, I laughed. "Ha-ha! Of course I'm with you—I was the one who came to you, remember?" I said. I knew I could count on my friends to help me out.

W.I.T.C.H. It's our initials—Will, Irma, Taranee, Cornelia, and me, Hay Lin. And even though we are not witches like the ones in books, with warts and funny hats and broomsticks or magic spells, W.I.T.C.H. is still a nice, handy name for what we do and who we are.

Specifically, we are Guardians of the Veil. A wise being known as the Oracle endowed each of us with her own power, which is supposed to help protect the world. I was given power over air. Which is fitting, since I'm the most flighty of the group. I'm always running around with my head in the clouds and a thousand thoughts in my mind. I am also the only one who has the ability to fly—a major perk of having power over air!

Irma, the most fluid of us, gets to play with water. Taranee heats things up with fire, and Cornelia controls the power of the earth. Will is our leader and has the strangest power of all—she unites all of our elements in pure energy. All the elements are held together in the Heart of Candracar, a special orb of intense power.

Our individual powers let us do all sorts of interesting and spectacular things. Cornelia can make solid objects move, which is great when you need to open locks or make class bells ring at the perfect moment, like when your teacher has just asked you a question and you have no clue what the answer is. And Will's power gives her a special power over electrical things—all of the household appliances in her home talk to her. It's pretty funny to hear Will get scolded—by her refrigerator! Taranee can create and control fire, so it's never dark or chilly when she is around. So, when we get together, we are strong enough that we can actually save the world—which we've had to—a couple of times.

With all that power, you'd think ordinary, everyday life would be a breeze. It isn't. In fact, getting through the daily stuff can be a nightmare. But at least I have a group of friends who under-stand me, friends to talk to and laugh with, and friends who would stand up for me and fight for me, if they had to.

€ € ▲ ◎ €

After school, the five of us went over to the China Shop.

"It doesn't look all that magical," said Irma with a hint of disappointment in her voice as we stood outside the shop.

"I know, but trust me. Something felt funny," I said, aware that the China Shop looked solidly unmagical, and that the wind chimes that had lured me into it that morning were gone. This time, when we opened the door, there was just a boring, electronic *bing-bong*. The inside of the store was dark, and there was nothing there that resembled the mirror I had picked up earlier. Behind the counter, a man looked up.

"Good afternoon," he said, without sounding as though he meant it. "May I help you?"

He didn't look anything like the young woman who had helped me earlier that morning. His expression was cold, and his eyes looked empty.

Startled, I paused for a moment before speaking. "I was here this morning," I explained. "I bought this mirror." I brought the mirror out and unwrapped it. "Only I didn't have any . . ."

"You didn't buy that here," he said, interrupting me.

"But I spoke to this woman. . . ." I started to explain.

"We don't deal in secondhand merchandise," he said abruptly, cutting me short once more. "If you're looking for a refund, I'm sorry, but I really can't help you."

A refund? What was this man talking about? Who said anything about a refund?

"I'm not looking for a *refund*," I said. "This morning . . ."

"We're not open in the mornings. I told you, you must have the wrong shop."

He looked at us sternly, waiting for us to leave. There wasn't much else we could do, so we turned and left the store.

Outside in the street, Irma shrugged her shoulders. "This keeps getting weirder," she muttered. "Either *you* are totally losing it—which . . ." she added with a sly grin, ". . . is of course a distinct possibility, or, there is something *very* strange going on here."

I just stood outside the shop, holding the mirror tightly to me. My eyes were tearing up, and I had a funny feeling in my chest, as if I had lost something and didn't know how to find it again. I think some part of me thought I would find my grandmother in the shop, even though I knew that was impossible.

"Are you all right, Hay Lin?" asked Taranee, linking her arm gently through mine. Her glasses slipped down her nose, and she pushed them back up. "You look pretty sad."

"I'm okay. It's just . . . I'm so worried about Uncle Kao, and I . . ." I wanted to say that I missed my grandmother terribly. But I couldn't bring myself to say it. So, instead, I said, "Well, I . . . I'm just worried, is all."

"Can I see the mirror for a second?" asked Will, trying to break up the mood of sadness.

I hesitated, not ready to let the mirror go quite yet. Then I handed it to her. It was heavy, and the frame was tarnished and nearly black with age. It was decorated with four crescent moons, inlaid with something that looked like pearl.

"I'm not sure you should take this home with you," said Irma. "What if it has some sort of dangerous magic connected to it? I mean, look at the way you found it."

I shook my head. "It's not dangerous," I said, with more conviction than I felt. "No more dangerous than the Heart." I wasn't quite sure what made me compare the mirror to the Heart of

Candracar. Maybe it was the feeling that the mirror, too, had some strong, good magic about it.

"But the Heart can be quite dangerous," Will pointed out. "Especially if you don't know what you're doing."

"True," I said. "But it's not ever willingly harmful. If the mirror is somehow connected to my grandmother, it won't harm me."

"If there is something magical about it," said Taranee, "we should be able to figure that out."

"Maybe it's a scrying mirror," said Irma. Then she posed as if holding a microphone and started to talk like a salesperson. "This mirror also serves as a handy flat-screen monitor that will make crystal balls obsolete. Look through it and see the future! Its compact, state-of-the-art, user-friendly design makes it the scrying device of choice."

Taranee giggled. "Well, I could certainly use a little help with my scrying technique! I never can seem to get the whole image in a mirror."

"Hanabaker Park is not too far from here," Cornelia said. "Why don't we go there and see if that's really what this thing is?"

Looking around, I saw all my friends nodding enthusiastically. My heart swelled with pride and love. I was so lucky to have friends like them to help me out.

It didn't take us long to get to the park. The warm spring day had lured a lot of joggers and skaters outside, but we still managed to find a quiet spot away from the crowds. I laid the mirror flat on the ground so that the misty old glass caught the bright sunlight as much as possible.

"Who wants to go first?" I asked.

"I'll go," said Irma. As the group's water baby, she had been the first of us to try scrying. While she loved it, I was much happier drawing things or sketching out images and places we saw. So I liked to leave the scrying stuff to Irma. Usually it worked best with water—but mirrors were good, too.

"It definitely should be Irma," Will agreed. "She's better at it than any of us."

With an extravagant gesture, Irma began. "Mirror, mirror, on the ground . . ." said Irma, leaning over the clouded glass. "Show us where your secret is. . . ."

"Very clever," said Cornelia. "You're such a poet!"

"Please! I need silence." Irma raised her hands dramatically.

Despite the impressive gestures and the frown of concentration on Irma's brow, the mirror showed no more than a glimpse of sky.

"Nothing?" I asked after a while.

"Nothing," Irma replied glumly. "I guess it's not a scrying mirror after all."

Taranee thoughtfully rubbed the pearly decorations. "It's got moons on it," she said. "Maybe it only does whatever it's supposed to do, if it does anything at all, at night. By moonlight."

"It's worth a try," Will said, getting up and brushing a few leaves from her jeans. "Maybe we should try again tonight."

"I've got skating practice tonight," said Cornelia. Cornelia is a great skater and never misses a practice meet if she can help it.

"And I have to go to the hospital with my dad to see Uncle Kao," I said.

"Well, then, what about tomorrow night? Do you think it has to be a full moon, or something?" Will asked.

I remembered what Uncle Kao had said about "the right time."

"The moons on the mirror are crescent moons," I said. "Not full. So I don't think we have to wait for a special night."

"True. So, do you want to try tomorrow?" Will asked with a smile on her face.

"Might as well," I replied. I wanted this mystery solved more than anyone did. And I wanted it solved soon. Very soon.

⬯ ⬯ ⬯ ⬯ ⬯

At the hospital that night, Uncle Kao's breathing was worse, and he was unconscious the whole time we were there. I held his hand for a while, but it didn't seem to make any difference. The room was silent except for his breathing, and I found my gaze constantly drifting over to my sketch. It was still on the bedside table, the light from the overhead lamp throwing odd shadows all over the page. Again I thought of Uncle Kao's strange words and of the lady at the China Shop. I was getting more and more confused. Nothing made sense anymore. Grabbing my sketch, I squeezed Uncle Kao's hand one more time and quickly left the room.

Later that night, in my room, I stared up at the strange mirror, which was hanging on the wall behind the lantern. I had placed the mirror there, hoping it might give me a sign. When I finally fell asleep that night, I once again dreamed of the mountain, even more vividly than before. The details were very vivid. I could make out wind chimes and trees, and I heard a voice calling out, over and over again. In my dream, I opened my eyes and found that the lantern had been lit. And in the mirror, clear as day, I saw the mountain in a shimmer of sunlight. It all seemed so real.

When I woke up a little later, my room was quiet and dark, with no lantern light. But when I looked at the mirror, I seemed to see, just for a second, the reflection of a mountainside fading into the background.

4

The next night, memories of my dream still lingered. It was as if I hadn't fully woken up yet. That was not a good thing—I had a mission ahead of me.

Shaking off as much of my sleepiness as I could, I sneaked down the stairs with the lantern and the mirror clutched in my hands. I was very careful not to make the steps creak. I didn't want my parents to wake up.

Will was waiting for me when I got to Hanabaker Park a little while later.

"Did you have any trouble getting out?" I whispered.

She shook her head and laughed. "Well," she said, "my *mother* didn't give me any trouble."

"So who did?" I asked.

She grinned. "James told me I was behaving

'most improperly.' He's so formal."

James is Will's refrigerator. Like every other appliance in her household, he talks to her—usually offering advice on proper behavior and eating habits. He sounds more like an old English nanny than a refrigerator!

"Good thing he didn't wake up your mother," I said.

"No kidding," said Will, nodding her head in agreement. Then she laughed. "Can you imagine? I'd have to explain why I was sneaking out and why our refrigerator speaks! It would definitely be awkward."

Just then, Taranee came in through the gate, followed by Cornelia and Irma. "Sorry I'm so late," Irma said when the group met up. "My dad has the night shift at the police station, and I had to wait until he'd left before I could leave. It took him forever!"

Irma's father is a sergeant on the Heatherfield police force. Irma got her detective skills from him—and from watching her favorite TV show, *Spygirl*.

"Don't worry about it. At least you managed to get here," I said. "And now that we're *all* here, I say we get down to business."

We gathered under a large cherry tree. The

night was a little cold, and I felt myself shiver. Actually, I wasn't sure if it was the cold or the idea of what we were about to do that had brought about the chill. I wrapped my arms around myself and took a deep breath. I couldn't afford to be scared.

"Let's hang the lantern here," suggested Will, snapping me out of my internal freak-out. "And the mirror, too. I think we'll need both."

I nodded. Like Will, I had a feeling that the moon mirror and Liu's lantern were connected. Carefully, I tied the lantern to one slender branch of the cherry tree. Cornelia held the mirror up while Taranee tied it to the branch Will had pointed to.

"Hold on just a sec," said Cornelia. She leaned forward and looked closely at the mirror. "I see something. . . . There's something on the back of it."

Carefully, she rubbed the mirror with her sleeve. This left a dark smear on her very fashionable jacket, but she didn't seem to care. She was too busy looking at the mirror.

"Look," she said, in an awed whisper. "The back is a mirror, too!"

We all gasped. Slowly, I turned the mirror around to look. Cornelia was right. The mirror had been so tarnished and black that the mirroring on the back hadn't been noticeable at first. But with a bit more rubbing, it became obvious that this was, in fact, a two-sided mirror. By that point, nothing could surprise me. Whatever wild-goose chase my Uncle Kao had sent us on was definitely going to test all of our keen W.I.T.C.H. senses. I was sure this was not the last of the surprises we'd see on our adventure.

"This side has suns on the rim," Taranee pointed out a moment later, after looking over Cornelia's shoulder. "The mirror has both a sun face and a moon face."

"Are we supposed to know what that means?" asked Irma. "I thought the whole reason we were out now is that it worked by moonlight, and now there are suns, too! This doesn't make any sense!"

Irma was right. It *didn't* make sense. But we couldn't stop now. I looked up at the night sky. It was completely clear and unclouded, full of bright stars and a huge, pale-yellow moon. My eyes drifted back to the lantern. In the darkness, I could just make out the vague shape of the mountain and the cheerful sun smiling down on it. Suddenly, I had an idea.

"Hey! Can we try something? Hang the mirror

so the moon side of the mirror is toward the moon," I said, pointing to the object Cornelia still clutched in her hands. "Then hang the lantern so that it shines on the sun side of the mirror."

Will listened and slowly nodded. "I think I see what you're trying to do," she said. "It will allow the sun and the moon to exist at the same time!"

In no time, we had hung both the mirror and the lantern from the dark cherry-tree branches; they bobbed gently in the wind.

"Taranee," I said, "could you light the lantern? And please be careful. It's very old. If anything happens to it . . ." My voice trailed off as I imagined the disappointed look in Uncle Kao's eyes. I couldn't bear hurting him.

Taranee smiled gently at my anxiety. "I haven't set anything on fire in ages," she said. "Well, I mean, anything I didn't want to have catch fire, that is. I think your lantern is safe with me."

Reassured, I backed away so that she could light the candle.

Taranee closed her eyes for a brief moment. Instantly, a tiny flame appeared inside the old lantern. And then, something else started to happen.

"Look!" said Irma softly.

With the lantern lit, the mirror had begun to glow. A mountain appeared. I couldn't believe my eyes. It was the mountain from my dreams!

And then I heard it. Very clearly, I could make out the sound of wind chimes, and a girl's voice, calling.

A thin, pleading voice that I could just barely hear said, "Help us in our need!"

I looked at the others.

"Did you hear that?" I whispered. "It sounded like an old woman."

My friends all nodded.

"I don't know if that's a good thing," Irma quipped. "It could mean we are *all* officially losing it!"

Cornelia was in no mood to put up with Irma. "Oh, be quiet! This is not the time for jokes, Irma. Listen!"

The voice was pleading even more fiercely than before, and I jumped in surprise. "You made a promise! We need you!" it said. "Don't desert us."

A promise? What promise? I hadn't made any promises. Unless . . . promising to pay for the mirror was what the voice meant. I thought back to what I had said that day in the China Shop.

"I always keep my promises," I had told the woman in the shop. And the woman had answered, "Good. That is important." Did this voice have some connection with my earlier words?

It didn't matter. I couldn't ignore that desperate voice. No one could have.

"We have to help her," I said urgently.

"You don't even know who's calling you," said Cornelia. "It could be a trap."

"But she seems to know me," I exclaimed. There was no way my friends were going to talk me out of this.

"That's even more reason to be suspicious," Cornelia remarked matter-of-factly.

I groaned silently. Leave it to Cornelia to raise the caution flag. Of all of us, Cornelia is the most skeptical, the hardest to convince. It made sense that she would control something solid—like the earth. Usually, that whole skepticism thing is a good thing for us, because it keeps us from charging off without thinking things through. But right then, I didn't want to listen to her logic. This was the moment to throw caution to the wind—in my case, literally!

"Whoever she is, she's in some kind of trouble. We need to help her!" I cried.

"We should ask the Oracle," suggested Taranee. "He'll know what we should do. Besides, how else will we get to her, if that's what we are supposed to do?"

Going to see the Oracle was something that really used to freak me out. He lives in Candracar, which is this overwhelmingly beautiful place, full of interesting creatures. And everyone there is aware that we are the Guardians of the Veil, with this huge responsibility. It's really intimidating. Luckily, the Oracle is cool. He's quiet and thoughtful and extremely kind. Just being around him makes all my fears vanish. He also seems to lead us in the right direction when it comes to Guardian problems. Which was why we were going to see him now.

Taranee had barely said the word, "Oracle" when the image in the mirror changed. Instead of the sunlit mountainside of before, there was a huge, pillared hall, stretching off into infinity. It was the Temple of Candracar. Standing in the hall, side by side, were the Oracle . . . and my grandmother.

My heart started beating wildly, and my eyes misted over. I could hardly see their two smiling faces through the tears that were beginning to well up in my eyes. But I could hear my grandmother's voice clearly. It felt as though she were standing right there next to me.

My heart filled with joy, and I wanted to reach out and hug her. Even though I knew she was just an image in the moon mirror, that image felt very real. I wanted to tell her everything—about my kite, Uncle Kao, my life . . . but we didn't have the time. I could tell this was not going to be a visit full of catching up on things. We had a job to do.

"Use the Heart, girls. Use the Heart," my grandmother said, interrupting my silent thoughts. Her voice was encouraging, urging us on, as if she knew we were hesitant to do what was required of us.

The image of Candracar faded. Once again, only moonlight filled the mirror. I felt a pang of sadness knowing that my grandmother had once again gone away. I took a deep breath to try and steady my racing emotions.

"Well, I guess we know what we have to do," Irma said excitedly. She loved it when we got to take action.

"Yes," said Will softly.

Cornelia nodded. "Yes. Let's go."

They looked at me. I nodded. If we were doing this, we were doing it together.

Will brought out the Heart of Candracar. The

Heart is always with her, but it's not always visible. The Heart, a crystal pendant caught in a silver clasp, comes to rest in her palm when she summons it. But this is no ordinary crystal—this crystal brings all our powers together and makes us as strong as we could be. It makes us W.I.T.C.H.!

"Should we transform first?" Will asked.

"I think we'd better," said Irma, for once being practical. "We have no idea what's going to happen once we call on the Heart to help us with our little mirror mystery."

Transforming is one of the cooler things about being a Guardian. I mean, normally you wouldn't catch me out of the house without my standard goggles and funky leggings. It's my trademark style. Everyone expects to see me making some funky fashion statement, and who am I to disappoint them?

In fact, all of us have unique styles that distinguish us even before we take on our W.I.T.C.H. personas. Taranee always has her hair in fun braids, while Will is usually in some version of her tomboy outfit—a hoodie sweatshirt and baggy pants. Cornelia is the fashion plate of the group, which means the transformation doesn't make her outfits all that different—just maybe a bit more revealing. And Irma—well, Irma just wears whatever brings her the most attention—especially from boys!

So, really, when we transform, we just become better versions of ourselves. And somehow we also come to look . . . somehow perfect. Not like supermodels or anything, but just a little more *mature* than usual. And on top of that, we have these really great outfits, which are super flattering—they even have wings! Although my wings are the only ones that actually function, which is a perk of having power over air, I guess.

But it's more than just the physical stuff. It's an emotional thing, too. I feel so much more confident. Like, nothing is too difficult or dangerous to do, no enemy so great they can't be beaten. It's a pretty great feeling. I sometimes get the same feeling when I'm working on a really great painting or something. But nothing compares to the first moments of transforming into my W.I.T.C.H. form—even the rush I get creating an amazing kite or a beautiful picture. Right now, going through the transformation especially helped ease the longing that the sight of my grandmother had given me. At least seeing her with the Oracle let me know that she was in a good place surrounded by warmth and love. And the visit had made me feel somehow closer to her, as if she were really watching over me. I wanted to make her proud.

With a smile on my face and an image of Grandma in my head, I gave in to the feeling that the first whoosh of transformation had inspired. A few minutes later it was over, and we all gazed around at the "new and improved" versions of ourselves.

We always have to stop and admire ourselves when we are finally "good to go." It's become kind of a tradition of ours. Another way to make the Guardian thing more "ours." And since we all have such unique styles in our everyday lives, it's fun for us to see one another "in uniform." It gives us common ground . . . and we look mighty fierce when we come up against all the baddies we face.

"Well, then, everybody ready?" Will asked. When we all nodded, she smiled. With a look of determination, she brought the Heart into the center of her palm. "Heart of Candracar, show us the way," she urged softly but clearly.

The Heart glowed, and the mirror frame's glow grew brighter before stretching into a slim oval, almost long enough to touch the ground. The mirror was no longer a mirror, but a doorway.

A doorway that clearly led to a different world.

"Are we ready?" asked Will.

Cornelia nodded, a little doubtful. "Yes," she said. "All ready to step off into the unknown once more. And, I might add, without a proper plan . . . again."

"How are we supposed to make plans when we are never sure what we're getting into in the first place?" asked Irma. She and Cornelia had a habit of never agreeing—on anything!

"We don't have time to argue," said Taranee. "I think the edges on this thing are beginning to shrink!"

Without another word, we stepped through. Me first, then Will, then the other three. We were stepping straight into the unknown.

5

We went straight from moonlight into sunlight. For a moment, I just stood there, blinking, listening to the now familiar sound of wind chimes.

Suddenly, there was a startled squeak, and a thin figure leaped up in front of me. Blinking in the bright sunshine, I made out a Chinese girl of about my age, wearing a faded blue cotton shirt and white calf-length pants. Her black hair was pulled into neat round buns just behind her ears. At her feet was a curious collection of objects—a small reed mat, on top of which rested a bowl filled with water, a few grains of rice, some white flowers, and a clumsily drawn picture of a face.

"Is it really you?" the girl asked me.

"My name is Hay Lin," I said, "and these are my friends."

The girl bowed low to my friends and me.

"Welcome, and welcome also to your friends," she said.

"Who are you?" I asked. "And where, exactly, are we?"

"I'm Hua," she answered. "But people call me Petal. And we are on the White Wind Mountain, of course. Down there is the Valley of the Slow Willow River. Don't you recognize it?"

I looked toward the place she was pointing at. "No," I said slowly. "I'm pretty sure I've never been here before."

Hua's face dropped. She looked terrified.

"Oh, no," she wailed. "I've done it wrong. I've done it all wrong!" Without another word, she spun on her heel and took off down the path.

I barely caught the words that followed, but it sounded as if she said, "She'll get me, she'll get me for this!"

"Hua!" I called. "Petal . . . wait!"

I looked back at my friends and saw that Will had picked up Petal's bowl. It was blue and white, with a pattern of bending willows.

"What do you think she was doing with this?" Will asked. "There's water, rice, flowers."

"Maybe it's some kind of welcome," said Taranee. Then she added, "Or maybe she was trying to do some kind of magic."

Whatever it was, the whole setup looked fragile. The bowl was chipped, and there were only a few grains of rice. The scene made me sad.

"It doesn't look very . . . professional," Irma said, stating the obvious.

"She brought us here. I know she did," I said, feeling an odd urge to stand up for the girl. "And she succeeded. I would call that professional."

"But then she just ran off," Irma pointed out.

"I'm not surprised. I don't think she was expecting five of us. Maybe that was what she meant when she said she had done it all wrong," I said, unwilling to give up.

Will looked thoughtfully down at the bowl in her hands. Quietly, she spoke up. "She said, 'She'll get me for this.' Who do you think the *she* is?"

"I don't know," I replied. Another one of the objects on the ground caught my attention. It was a picture. From a distance it seemed to be just a clumsily drawn figure, but something made me peer at it more closely. I picked up the piece of white parchment and gasped.

It was a picture of a woman with long, dark hair and a warm smile. Her eyes shone brightly and she looked very familiar.

She looked like my grandmother.

"I need to find Petal," I said. I put the picture in my pocket and turned toward the trail down which Petal had gone. We had to find her. I needed some answers.

We followed the trail down the mountain. Hot sun shimmered on the rocks, and I could hear cicadas all around us.

Will suddenly yelled and swatted at her neck.

"Ouch!" she cried. "The bugs around here are horrible!"

"Yeah. There's so many of them," agreed Irma.

They were right. Flies and gnats and thirsty mosquitoes filled the air in the midday heat. There was a steady buzz and hum augmenting the loud noise made by the cicadas. But what was even weirder was the fact that there were no birdcalls, I suddenly realized.

"Have you all noticed there are no birds?" I asked. "Have you seen any? Or heard any?"

"Not a single one," replied Will, looking at the empty sky. "Am I the only one thinking that that may be a bad sign?"

None of us said a thing. It was definitely a bad sign.

After a while, we made it down the mountain

into what I assumed was the Valley of the Slow Willow River. It was easy enough to figure out. There, in the middle of a valley, was a slow-moving river surrounded by willow trees. Across the river there was a narrow wooden bridge, and beyond the bridge, a town.

"This place looks like it could use a good spring cleaning," Irma said.

"It looks like it's deserted, too," Taranee said.

It was true. The area looked as though it might have been prosperous at one time, but now many of the houses were boarded up, and weeds were growing in the gardens. On a hot day like that, there should have been plenty of people out on their porches, talking or simply sitting quietly. We saw nobody. It was as if we had stepped right into a ghost town.

"Hello?" Will called out, into the eerie silence. "Anybody here?"

I was shocked when somebody actually answered.

"Over here. I think I'm the only one around."

I turned toward the voice and saw an old woman wearing a bright kimono. She was sitting cross-legged in the doorway of a large house. As we moved closer, she turned toward us.

But something was strange about this woman.

Even though she was facing us, her eyes were looking to the left of us. That was when I realized she couldn't actually see us.

I glanced around at the others and, from the expressions on their faces, knew they had had the same realization. The woman was blind.

"Where is everyone?" Taranee asked the old woman gently. "Why are you here all alone?"

"You must be new here, or you would know where everyone is," the woman said slowly. "We haven't had visitors for a long time. Have you come here to see the empress—I mean, Her Celestial Majesty, the beauteous Song Ho?"

"We don't know Her Majesty," Will replied. She looked as confused as I felt.

A look of hope flashed across the old woman's face. Then, just as quickly, it was replaced by a blank stare. "Here in Slow Willow Town we know Her Majesty well," the woman explained. "That's where everyone is. They've gone to serve the empress. . . ." her voice trailed off.

"Everyone?" Irma asked in surprise. Even she, who was usually the first one to crack a joke, seemed perplexed by this announcement.

The old woman nodded. "Men, women, children . . . all serve Her Majesty in their own way. Except for those of us who are truly useless, of course. My granddaughter is there right now. It will be a while now before Petal comes back."

"Petal is your granddaughter?" I asked, remembering the girl who had greeted us earlier.

Until that moment, I hadn't spoken. But when the old woman heard my voice, she sat up stick straight and turned in my direction. Her sightless eyes bored into me, and for a moment I felt as though she actually saw me.

"Is that you?" she said, reaching out a hand desperately. It was shaking. "You came back! But why did you stay away for so long?"

Suddenly I understood what was happening. Why Petal seemed to know me. Why there was a picture of a woman who looked exactly like my grandmother sitting on a girl's mat on the mountainside. I gently took the old woman's hand in mine. "I think you have mistaken me for my grandmother, Yan Lin. *My* name is Hay Lin. I have come to help you now."

Briefly, the old woman's shoulders slumped, as if the news were too much for her to handle. Then she straightened up once more and smiled. "Welcome, then, young Hay Lin," she said kindly. "Please, come inside. There is much we have to talk about."

Sighing, the woman stood up and went inside.

We silently followed her, each of us trying to figure out what kind of world we had stepped into.

"You can call me Mama Liu," said the old woman once we had settled into seats in her shabby, but cozy, living room. "Everyone does. And please, tell me all of your names. It helps me picture you better." Smiling, Mama Liu listened as we introduced ourselves. When we had finished, she took a deep breath.

"Well, I bet you are trying to figure out why you are all here. I'm going to tell you, but it is a long story—so you'll have to be patient." Taking another deep breath, Mama Liu began. "When your grandmother first came to us, Hay Lin, we needed her help. Our valley had always been a peaceful place, until a cruel spirit arrived. She told us she was our empress and then demanded we work for her until our bodies and souls were broken. Just when things looked hopeless, your grandmother arrived. The struggle was bitter, but your grandmother used her magic wisely. In the end, the empress was banished from the Valley of the Slow Willow River." Mama Liu paused, and in the silence, we heard a low buzzing noise. It sounded like the buzzing of bugs' wings.

"What's that sound?" Taranee asked softly.

"Are all of the screens closed?" asked Mama Liu, ignoring Taranee's question.

"Yes. They are definitely closed," Cornelia replied, pushing on the screen closest to her.

Mama Liu sighed and pressed a slender hand against her forehead. I noticed that it was trembling slightly. Then she began speaking again. "That was a great moment," she said. "The people of Slow Willow Town were proud and joyous. We were convinced that everything was better. But then your grandmother had to leave us. She said she would come back if she were needed, but she never did. And we need her now. The Cruel Empress has returned, and she is determined to ruin the Valley of the Slow Willow River."

The buzzing outside had grown louder, and a sharp rapping noise had joined it.

"What *is* that?" Taranee repeated, a little more forcefully this time.

I started to say I didn't know, but Mama Liu interrupted me.

"It's insects," she said. "They're hitting the screens."

I couldn't believe my ears. Mama Liu must have been crazy. If those were bugs, then they sounded super mad. I looked around and noticed that my four friends were not liking the sound of this. They were huddled together, looking at the screens apprehensively.

Suddenly, Mama Liu's voice rose above the roar. "Did I say, 'the Cruel Empress'?" she asked. "I misspoke. I humbly apologize. I meant, of course, Her Celestial Majesty, the beauteous Song Ho. Blessed be her name!"

At first, nothing happened. Then, with a crack, the paper screen split down the middle. A swarm of gnats, thick as smoke, poured into the room and headed straight for Mama Liu. The old woman crouched down on the floor and wrapped her arms around her head to protect her face.

I jumped to my feet. I couldn't stand by and watch Mama Liu be attacked.

Using my Guardian power I summoned up a gust of wind and tried to make the gnats drift away from Mama Liu, but it didn't work. There were too many of them. Irma tried drenching the pests with rain. But still they didn't leave. When the swarm eventually scattered and disappeared, I felt it was more because someone had called them off than because we had defeated them.

I rushed over to Mama Liu's side. "Are you hurt?" I asked. Mama Liu was still crouched down, her hands covering her eyes.

Slowly, she lowered her hands. Her face was swollen from the bug bites, but otherwise she looked okay.

"Are they really gone?" she asked quietly.

"Yes. They've all left," I replied.

Mama Liu let out a bitter laugh. "Now you can see why no one sticks around. I used to think there wasn't much she could do to an old woman like me, but I was wrong." She gently rubbed at one of the swollen spots on her arm. "Those bugs are her servants. They are her eyes and ears. If you offend Her Majesty, they will hear it, and they'll punish you. If you try to rebel against Her Majesty, you will not sleep peacefully until she gets her revenge. After a while, people will do anything to avoid this cruel punishment." Mama Liu's voice shook, and tears welled up in her eyes as she continued. "When she first came here . . . I tried to stand up to her, thinking somebody had to. And she took my sight. Now all I see is the swarm. Black wings. Nothing except the blackness of wings." She shuddered. "Now, I can no longer look at Petal's face. And the Cruel Empress? She's still there, ruining our lives."

With a huge sigh, Mama Liu grew quiet.

I looked around at the sad faces of my friends and knew we had to do something.

6

Seeing the grief on Mama Liu's face was heart-wrenching. She looked devastated, and, even worse, she looked hopeless. The thought of her never seeing Petal's face or even a sunset filled me with anger.

Usually I never get angry. As I've said before, I'm more a go-with-the-flow kind of girl. After all, if I let my anger take control all the time, things would get quite windy. Instead, I like things to go smoothly, and I hate fighting. But this time I was livid, and all I wanted to do was take the empress down—just as my grandmother had done before me.

"We can't let this continue," I said, barely keeping the rage out of my voice. "I want to teach this empress how to treat people. It's about time she got a lesson in manners—a big one!"

Mama Liu smiled. "That's a lesson we would all like to teach her," she said. Then she added wistfully, "But it is far more easily said than done, child. The empress is strong, as you know. And not easily fooled."

I looked at my friends' concerned expressions and Mama Liu's sad one. There was no way I was going to take no for an answer.

"Where does the empress live?" I asked Mama Liu.

"Bird Cage Palace. It's up the river from here," she replied.

"Then I think that's where we should be heading," I said boldly. "And we need to get going—now. You guys coming with me?"

"Of course we are," said Will instantly. "We're your backup, remember?"

"It might be a good idea to get directions first," Cornelia pointed out.

"Well, since you girls are so determined," said Mama Liu, getting to her feet slowly, "we shall go see Her Majesty."

"We? Mama Liu, you can't. . . ." I had nearly said, "You're too old," but a fierce streak in her sightless old eyes stopped me before the words made it out of my mouth.

The time had come. Without another word,

we headed up the river. Mama Liu's thin, wrinkled hand rested on my arm as we walked. We were off on another adventure—I just hoped we would know how to win once we got to the end of the path.

❸ ❷ ▲ ⊙ ❻

It was pretty easy to figure out how Bird Cage Palace had gotten its name. Everywhere you looked, there were cages. Thousands of them. Hanging from trees, or from slender silver poles that looked like lampposts. The smallest were so tiny I could have wrapped my hands around them, while the largest would have housed a family of five. Some were made of gold and silver wire, others from slender bamboo, painted white or black. But although they all looked different, they had one thing in common. Inside every single one, captive birds perched, listlessly singing and chirping.

Seeing creatures who were born to play in the air—to dip, soar, and climb in the sky—trapped stirred up even more anger inside me. I thought of the moments when I took to the air and was truly free. It was an amazing feeling to soar above others with nothing holding me back. My heart ached for these birds, which so clearly needed that freedom. I took a deep breath and pulled my gaze away from the cages for a moment.

"So this is where all the birds went," I whispered, turning to Irma. "Remember how we thought it was pretty strange that there were no birds around when we got here?"

Irma nodded. "It was definitely weird, but all these cages are even weirder," she said.

For a moment, we were all silent as we looked around. The caged birds seemed to fill all of us with an inexplicable sadness. Sighing, we moved closer.

After a few minutes, we found ourselves in what appeared to be the palace gardens. They were enormous, and stunningly beautiful. Large trees bent gracefully over winding streams. Thousands of delicate shrubs and flowers filled the air with a wonderful smell. Compared to the sad spectacle of the caged birds, the sight of the gardens was oddly uplifting.

There were no walls or guards around the gardens. The Cruel Empress didn't need any. Her buggy servants were everywhere, and we felt their eyes on us as we wandered through the trees and flowers.

A young man was kneeling by a cluster of rosebushes, carefully pruning the flowers.

I stared at him, watching his fingers nimbly

separating the dead leaves from the healthy ones. I noticed that the man's hands were crisscrossed with little scratches from working on the thorny stems, and he had a look of deep concentration on his face. He didn't look up as we approached.

"Excuse me," I said quietly.

Surprised at the interruption, he glanced up at us. For a moment, hope seemed to flicker across his face. But it vanished instantly, and he quickly bent back over the roses.

"I have to work," he said. "I don't have time to talk."

"I was just wondering. . . ." I started to say.

"No time to talk," he repeated, snipping away with greater urgency.

Talk about some bad manners, I thought. This boy clearly had never gotten a lecture from my grandma about speaking politely to people.

Mama Liu, who had been extremely quiet up until that moment, took a deep breath. "Young Han, is that you?" she asked.

The young man stopped snipping again. "Yes, Mama Liu," he said, with a note of sadness in his voice. His hands were trembling.

"What are you doing here, ruining your hands with gardening, when you should be painting?" Mama Liu looked like a mother scolding her child. Turning to us, she explained, "He does the most beautiful paintings."

"I must do the work the empress demands," he said. "You should not be here. It will anger her. You should just go home, Mama Liu." He turned his attention back to the roses.

"I will," she replied. "When I've finished what I came here to do."

He gave her a frightened look. "Please, Mama Liu, don't do anything silly. . . . Just go home." His request was uttered in a whisper, and his eyes pleaded with her. It was as though he knew it was too late to change the old woman's mind.

Mama Liu sighed. "Can you at least tell me where I can find my granddaughter?"

"She's in the peach groves," he answered. "South of the Drifting-Snow Bridge."

Mama Liu nodded, and, looking at him sadly once more, we left him and headed for the southerly reaches of the gardens. Since we didn't know our way around, we silently followed Mama Liu.

A little farther up the path we came upon a boy. He was holding a basketful of seeds and trying to feed one of the birds. He chirped to it, then cooed to it and finally tapped his fingernail against the bars of the cage. But the swallow inside seemed completely uninterested in the boy *and* his food.

"Please eat," he said pleadingly. "Eat, or you will be sick."

I looked into the cage. I didn't want to say it, but the swallow looked as if it were already sick. It simply sat there, its head and wings drooping. It looked about as interested in the seeds as I was in homework.

The sight of the young boy trying to feed the sick bird was heartbreaking. I felt my eyes well up with tears. This whole place was so depressing.

Will must have felt the same way, because she walked quietly up to the boy. "I don't think he likes seeds," she told the boy softly, putting a gentle hand on his shoulder.

"I know," he said. "But he isn't allowed to eat bugs. Eating Her Majesty's servants is wicked." He looked into the cage and pointed his finger at the bird. "Wicked bird," he said. "Wicked, wicked bird." It was pretty obvious to us that he loved the "wicked" bird a lot.

"So what's up with all the cages?" Irma asked.

I was surprised she hadn't said anything up till then. It wasn't like her to be so quiet or to keep her snippy remarks to herself. But this place was having a weird effect on all of us.

The boy stopped tapping the bars and then tried to get the swallow's attention by holding up a sunflower seed. When that still didn't work, he turned to Irma. "They have to be locked up, or they would kill and eat the servants of the empress," he told her. "The empress commands us to cage them. She says it's for our own good."

Suddenly, it all made sense. The servants were insects, and all the captive birds were insect-eaters. No wonder the empress kept them locked up. If they got out, she would become instantly powerless.

"But if you only feed them seeds, they'll starve," said Will. "Don't you know that?" She looked sadly at the caged bird. Will was an animal lover, and seeing all those miserable birds was probably hard for her.

The little boy looked just as sad as she did. "But they *have* to learn," he said. "If I can teach them all to eat seeds, maybe Her Majesty will let them go, because then they won't eat her bugs any more."

It was clear the boy needed to believe that. But the hopelessness of his task made my heart ache.

"Maybe you're right," I told him, knowing deep down he wasn't.

We continued on our way to the Drifting-Snow Bridge. The bridge was surrounded by cherry and tulip trees, and when the wind blew, falling white petals made it look as if the area had been caught in a permanent blizzard.

"Whoever names these places sure goes for the obvious," Irma said sarcastically. The rest of us laughed, desperate for something to lighten the mood.

Beyond the bridge lay the peach groves we had been looking for. Fat wasps buzzed around piles of neatly gathered fruit. All over the grove, people were working, tending to the trees, and occasionally laying out more peaches for the greedy insects to devour. I saw Petal among the workers.

"There's your granddaughter," I told Mama Liu.

"Are there any others with her?" the old woman asked hopefully.

"Around thirty or so," I told her. I was actually more surprised to see that many of the workers were so young. It seemed like such an odd job for *anybody*—feeding bugs—but it seemed an even weirder task for kids.

"Hmmm. That's not enough," Mama Liu said

thoughtfully. "We need all the help we can get. Perhaps others will join us on the way to the palace."

"You want to bring all these people with us?" Will asked, shocked. I think we had all assumed it was going to be a small group going up against the empress. Clearly, Mama Liu had another idea.

"We'll need them," Mama Liu said. "We are battling the servants of the empress, and sooner or later, they will wear us down. There is no end to their numbers, and we must get to the empress herself. We must make it past the bugs and get to the inner halls of the palace. For that, child, we need more than five girls and one old woman."

It occurred to me suddenly, that Mama Liu had this planned out much better than we did. I smiled. It was a good thing she had come along after all.

"But do you think anyone will come?" I asked, eyeing the obedient workers in the grove. "The empress seems to have everyone pretty scared."

"Oh, I think there is some spirit left in people. We just need to find it." Raising her voice, she called out, "Petal! Petal, my dear, come and lend your old grandmother an arm."

Startled to hear her grandmother's voice so far from the safety of their home, Petal dropped the weed basket she was carrying and ran over. "Grandmother! What are you doing here?" she asked breathlessly when she reached us.

"Hay Lin thought it was time to teach the empress a lesson. I came to help," Mama Liu said proudly.

"Grandmother! You shouldn't talk like that!" Petal said, looking around wildly, her pretty, heart-shaped face filled with anxiety.

I quickly realized why Petal looked so worried. Mama Liu's voice had roused the wasps. A swarm of them rose up from the fruit piles, buzzing dangerously. Before they could do anything, I sent a quick blast of wind their way, scattering them. Unfortunately, some shot off in the direction of the palace—gone to report to the empress.

Even though she couldn't see what was happening, Mama Liu knew enough to lower her voice. She turned to me. "Hay Lin, could you do something? Protect us in some way so I can speak to my neighbors without being interrupted?" she asked quietly.

"I can," replied Will, jumping in before I could say or do anything. It looked like Will was in full-on leader mode. And when that happened, watch out! "It should just take a minute," she predicted.

Sure enough, we were soon all encased by a thin globe of blue-edged, pearly light. Petal and her fellow laborers gasped in wonder. Some of the wasps that had been caught inside with us flew straight at the pearly light, and then plopped down into the grass, stunned. The others, which turned on the humans, Irma doused with raindrops.

I was feeling pretty proud of my friends. Then, just as I was about to say something encouraging, I heard a few people mutter something that sounded like "foreign demons," but Mama Liu quickly silenced them.

"Stop talking nonsense," she told the group. "These girls have traveled far to help us, and we should welcome them with gratefulness, not insult them with talk of demons! Don't you want to get back to your old lives? There is nothing wrong with growing fruit, but growing fruit only to feed the wasps and their cruel mistress is a senseless job for grown men and women with your skills!"

People were listening now, and they drew slowly closer to us.

"You make it sound as if defeating the empress is an easy task," said a large, mild-faced man. Petal whispered in my ear that he was called Wu the Carpenter. "But we all know it isn't," the man continued. "We all know it's impossible."

"No, it may not be easy, but impossible? I don't believe that," Mama Liu said. "Look at the globe keeping her servants at bay as we speak. Are they not a mighty magic? Once before, with the help of such strong magic, we defeated the Cruel Empress. I think we can do it again. And I say we must *try*. Better to try and fail than to live forever as her slaves, not even *hoping* for a better life!"

The effect of Mama Liu's words was amazing. Petal slipped her hand under her grandmother's arm, her eyes shining with pride. I felt a pang of jealousy. I wished my grandmother were there, too.

"But . . . how can we do this?" asked a young girl who was not much older than Petal.

"We will have to fight our way into the palace," said Mama Liu. "We can go through the Great Dragonfly Gates to reach the empress. We must capture her to end the battle and put an end to her cruel reign. We cannot wait any longer."

There was a collective gasp as the group understood the magnitude of the task that lay before them. Fear filled their eyes.

"But she'll send her servants after us. They'll sting us, bite us. There are so many of them!" said one of the workers.

"*You* don't have to defeat them. You just have to help us get through to the empress," I said. "Then we can take care of the rest. It's what we came here to do. No harm will come to you if we can help it."

Wu the Carpenter let out a bitter laugh. "We just have to help you get through," he said, as if this were a huge joke. "So simple."

"If we do capture her . . ." said a woman clutching a basket of peaches. "If we do capture her—then that will be the end of it? No more working in her gardens? No more pretending to admire her, and having to call her Her Beauteous Majesty? And no more stinging gnats and pestering flies and plagues of wasps if we fail to please her?"

"Never again," said Mama Liu confidently. "If we catch her, we *will* be free."

After hearing Mama Liu's promise, the rest of the group quickly agreed to help. With a group to help us, we now needed a plan—including a way to protect ourselves against the insects that were sure to attack us the minute Will lifted the protective globe. We needed to be prepared.

"Do you think you could move the globe?" asked Cornelia. "That way we could take it with us to the palace."

Will shook her head. "I don't think so. And even if I could, we wouldn't be able to see where we were going," she said, pointing out something we all knew was true.

"So we need some sort of movable defense," Cornelia, our planner, said with a thoughtful frown. "Mmmm. Maybe this will help."

Leaning down, she put her hand on the ground. I knew vaguely that she was calling on the powers of the earth to help her, but I had no idea what she was up to specifically. I didn't want to question her, though. I knew that Cornelia would do something impressive. At that moment, the soil erupted. Plant life poured forth like a fountain, and delicate green tendrils began shooting out in all directions. Suddenly the air was filled with the pungent smell of garlic.

"Jeez, Corny," said Irma, clutching her nose, "that stuff is really appetizing."

"That was the plan. Let's hope the insects don't like the stink either," Cornelia replied.

"Taranee, can you come over here for a sec?"

"Um . . . why?" Taranee asked hesitantly.

"I just think I should try it out on one of us first. To see what happens, you know," Cornelia answered.

Taranee gulped, but bravely stepped up to face the garlicsuckle, or whatever it was. At Cornelia's command, some of the shoots attached themselves to Taranee's body, weaving every which way until she was encased from head to toe in a sort of loose-fitting green armor.

"Does it hurt?" Cornelia asked once Taranee was "suited up."

"Nope," came Taranee's voice from inside the green suit. "It tickles, though. And the smell is definitely unappetizing."

"I think it will take a pretty stubborn bug to get through this," declared Cornelia. "What do you guys think?"

"Cool—bugproof armor," exclaimed Irma. "I like it a lot. Good job, Corny!"

Cornelia grinned. It wasn't all that often she got a compliment from Irma—a genuine compliment, that is.

"So . . . does anyone else want one?" she asked.

"I think it would be a good idea if we all wore

them," said Will. "Do you think that's possible, Cornelia? Suits for all the villagers—and all of us?" she asked hopefully.

"Don't see why not," said Cornelia.

"Well," said Irma, "at least we'll all smell equally awful."

Soon, the entire group was wrapped up in green. Looking around, I laughed. We were one funny-looking—not to mention smelly—group.

"Come on," Will said. "It's time we met the empress."

The battle was about to start.

The only question was, were we ready?

7

It didn't take long for the attack to begin. With a wave of Will's hand, the protective globe vanished, and a swarm of bugs immediately descended. There were flies, gnats, wasps, and bees longer than my thumb. Even though I had been expecting them, I was still shocked at the sheer number of them.

Cornelia's green outfits helped. The sharp smell of the garlic sent the swarm of bugs scattering. The reprieve didn't last long. The buggy army quickly regrouped for a second attempt. Down they came, managing somehow to stay together despite the powerful stench.

"Move," screamed Will. "Don't stop. Keep moving toward the palace!"

I looked around and tried to gauge our group's energy. Some looked scared senseless, while others, like Petal and Mama Liu, looked remarkably calm. Unfortunately, I didn't have time to offer comfort or words of encouragement to the group. The swarm was so dense now it looked like a huge fist aiming a blow at us.

It was time for me to use some of *my* magic.

"North wind," I whispered. "Blow these bugs away!"

Immediately, a cool blast of wind came rushing down off the mountain. The peach branches shuddered at the strength of it, and the buggy fist was blown apart. Some of the insects dropped to the ground, coated with glistening frost. Others vanished on the wind. I hoped it would be a while before they recovered or returned.

Slowly we made our way across the Drifting-Snow Bridge. Even as we moved forward, I kept my eyes on the sky, waiting for the next swarm to descend on us.

Suddenly, I felt a sharp bite on my ankle. I yelped and looked down. What I saw made me gasp. The ground was crawling with ants! Some of them were getting through our protective gear. I shifted from one foot to the other, trying to keep the persistent ants from biting me. I noticed that all around me, the others were doing the same dance. Clearly, the ants were the empress's next line of defense. She would take us down by bug-bite.

Then Cornelia's voice rang out, calm and collected. "Earth, take these bugs back!" I smiled at the thought of what Cornelia's reaction to a swarm of ants would be if we had been at home. I pictured a lot of shrieking.

Instantly, the soil beneath my feet shook. Dirt poured over the ants, burying them beneath our feet. I breathed a big sigh of relief. That is, until I looked up.

The sky had turned pitch black. Every sort of flying insect—beetles, flies, moths, striped hornets, locusts, anything that had a sting, a barb, or just the smothering weight of its wings for a weapon—was in the air above us. I cried out, warning the others.

There were too many of them for us to fight. We were cornered.

I could try to blow them away, but the sky was black with them. The moment I got rid of some, others would appear.

We needed more help.

Suddenly, I thought of the perfect solution to our problem. I smiled triumphantly and looked around, trying to find the person who could put an end to this buggy attack.

"Cornelia," I called. "Can you unlock the cages?" I knew that Cornelia had the power to open one lock just by thinking about it. I hoped that opening a thousand was sort of the same thing. If not, we were in trouble.

"I'll try," she replied. There was a moment of silence and then I heard some sharp little clicks coming from all around us. Cage doors were springing open, and dazed birds were suddenly face to face with freedom.

"Fly," I urged them. "Fly!"

There was a rushing, feathery surge, and then thousands of birds took to the air. Very hungry birds, I added silently to myself, with a feeling of hope.

Above us, the birds dipped and soared, their beaks flashing and snapping. It was like watching some strange 3-D video game. For every bug snapped up, I wanted to give someone a point. Soon the sky was no longer black but only smoky gray. Then Irma made a warm rain fall. To us, it was just a summer shower, but to the insects, the drops were large enough to feel like water bombs, dousing wings and making flight impossible.

"Take that!" Irma said with smug satisfaction, as her rainstorm got rid of the last of the swarm in a mighty *whoosh*.

All around I could hear sighs of relief from our little army. That had been a close call.

Satisfied that we were safe for the moment, we once again began to walk toward the palace. Soon we could see it in the distance. It was black and white against the blue-gray sky, with gold trim gleaming in the after-shower sunshine. And in front of the palace itself were the Great Dragonfly Gates.

But something was blocking our way through the gates.

Something with big, furry legs and a body bigger than a truck.

Something that sent a collective shiver down all of our spines.

"You've got to be kidding me," whispered Taranee next to me. "A spider? I hate spiders!"

"Anyone have any bug spray?" asked Irma. "Extra-strength would be great. And make sure it's the nonirritating stuff—I wouldn't want to get a rash." She was trying to keep her voice light and playful, but I could hear a tremble. Faced with that monster-sized tarantula, who could blame her? It was like a nightmare come to life.

"What is it?" Mama Liu asked, coming up beside me.

"A—a spider," Petal told her grandmother. "It's a spider the size of an elephant! And it's blocking the palace gates. There's no way for us to get past it—we've failed!"

I hated to see defeat in Petal's eyes. We couldn't turn back now. "Cornelia?" I said, looking at my earth-friendly friend. "Think you could take care of this, too? Maybe an earthquake? Just a very small one? Roughly spider-sized, if you know what I mean."

Cornelia nodded grimly and knelt down to place her palm flat on the ground. Once again, there was a slight rumble and tremor, but although the soil gaped open beneath the spider, the creature merely shifted its legs a bit and remained standing. I could have sworn the spider was laughing at our efforts.

"Try again," I said urgently.

Cornelia tried again with the same result.

"It's not working," she said. She sounded drained by her efforts. "I could try a bigger quake, but that might bring down the whole palace. Are there any people in there?"

"Yes," Mama Liu replied. "The empress loves attention. She always keeps a few people around to tell her how beautiful she looks. And there are also servants who keep everything spotless and perfect enough to satisfy her."

"Well, that answers that question. No quake," said Will firmly. "We can't risk destroying the palace or hurting any of the people inside. I'll try to zap the thing instead."

Ziiing.

Blue light flashed from her hand, like a miniature lightning bolt. Knowing the strength of Will's power, I expected to see the monster crumble instantly. But the lightning appeared to pass right through it with no effect whatsoever. It remained standing, giving us the cold, buggy eye.

Will looked perplexed. She wasn't used to her magic having no effect.

"What's that thing made of?" she asked. Her voice was filled with confusion and a little fear. My heart sank. Seeing your leader lose faith is always a depressing sight. Clearly, I wasn't the only one who was worried by Will's show of doubt.

"Please," begged Petal. "You must do something! That is the only entrance to the palace. If we stay here much longer, another swarm will gather. And this time there are no more birds to help us."

"Let me try," growled Taranee. "What do you say we try and warm things up a little?"

She leaned down, just as Cornelia had, and placed her hands gently on the ground. Beneath the giant spider the dirt started to steam, and flickering heat shimmered up and around its eight feet. In response, the beast began lifting first one foot, then another, then another. And then, it began to move . . . straight toward us!

At the sight of the approaching monster, most of the villagers turned and fled. I'm not going to lie—I felt like running, too. But I knew Mama Liu would never be able to move fast enough to escape the beast, and I couldn't leave her behind.

Without thinking, I unfolded my wings and flew into the air. I had waited long enough. It was my turn to do something. After all, this whole mission was kind of my fault. I owed it to my friends—and to Mama Liu—to take action.

Hovering just above the nasty beast, I hit it with a short, hard gust of wind, like a jab to the ribs. The monster turned, trying to figure out the direction from which the attack had come. I flitted out of its reach and jabbed it in another spot.

One of the beast's eight legs moved, bending at an angle no spider's leg should be able to bend at. It snagged one of my wings, jerking me quickly down into an uncoordinated tumble. I was going to fall right on top of it!

But I didn't—I kept falling. I fell right *through* the monster and hit the ground with a hard thump.

Dimly, I heard Taranee scream. Then I heard Irma call my name. Blue-edged light shimmered around me, and I knew Will was zapping the monster with all her strength.

But all I could think was, I had fallen *through* the spider. I was not on top of it or crushed underneath. I was *inside* it!

I felt something moving on my skin. And that something was biting me, although not with the huge, tearing bites that the monster would have bitten me with. These bites were ant-sting painful, not somebody-get-a-stretcher painful. And there was the creepy sensation of thousands of small furry legs crawling all over me. It took all my effort not to let out a bloodcurdling shriek.

I knew exactly what this thing was. It wasn't a spider. It was thousands of spiders, held together by the will of the empress in the shape of a giant tarantula.

I knew what I had to do. Keeping my mouth and eyes tightly shut, I focused all my energy on calling up my magic.

Blow, wind, I thought. Join forces with me and blow this creature far, far away!

In answer to my cry, wind howled around me, scattering the thousands of spiders in all directions.

It was a while before I dared to open my eyes. I was a little scared of what I might see. Images of my bug-bitten face flashed in front of me. They were *not* pretty.

"Hay Lin!" Irma cried, running over and touching my face and hands, trying to see if I were hurt. There was no sign left of the giant beast. "Are you all right?" Irma asked, looking worried.

"Yes," I replied. "My back's sore, and I have a few bites, but otherwise, I'm okay." Luckily, no major bites, I added silently. They would be hard to explain back home.

"What did you do to it?" Will asked. "It just . . . blew apart."

I grinned weakly. "Exactly. It wasn't really one big spider. It was *thousands* of little ones. . . . That was why your lightning passed right through it, Will. You stunned a few hundred of them, but the rest of them were unharmed. Same for your attempt to burn them, Taranee. It wasn't concentrated enough."

"When you fell . . ." Taranee took her glasses off and rubbed her eyes. Then she grabbed me and wrapped me in a huge hug. "Hay Lin, don't ever do that again! It was so scary!"

"Trust me," I said. "I'm not planning on repeating that experience. Now, let's get through those gates before Her Majesty gets creative again and sends something else after us!"

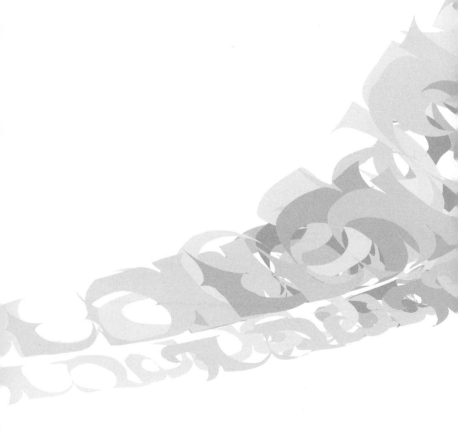

8

Since we became Guardians, we have seen our fair share of impressive palaces—but this one was breathtaking. It made the others look like dollhouses.

When all of the townsfolk and the five of us finally got through the gates and made our way into the building, we saw large pillars and beautiful sculptures. I felt my jaw drop as I stared at the grandeur of the place. It was like we had stepped into a fairy tale. But despite its beauty, the palace felt cold and unloved. And I couldn't shake the feeling we were being watched.

After getting our bearings, we moved further into the palace. There was another gate, and then we were walking into the throne room. What I saw there made me gasp.

It was so dark . . . and buggy! The floor was

pitch black, and it glittered with the wings of thousands of beetles. Every column in the room was a forest of wavering antennae and twitching legs. Every curtain on the windows was really a blur of gleaming dark wings.

In the middle of this sea of insect life stood the empress. She was just as I had imagined— cruel and regal. Her eyes were cold. She was tall and severe, her body covered by the swarm of whirring servants.

At the sight of the empress standing there, the townsfolk, who had boldly followed us in, now drew back helplessly. It was as if her presence took away all of the strength that had brought them there. Only Mama Liu and Petal stayed beside us. But despite her bravado, I could feel Mama Liu's fragile body trembling.

"Fools! What will you do now?" asked the empress in an icy voice. I shivered. "Your pesky birds can't come in here to save you, and you're outnumbered by my servants. I will offer you a deal that you would be wise to take. If you with-draw now, I *might* let you live."

"Don't believe a word she says," Mama Liu said boldly. "She is a liar! Her words mean noth-ing—they are as icy as her heart!"

"Ah! Is that Mama Liu? I thought I already

taught you a lesson once before. Why do you try to defy me again?" The empress asked with a cruel laugh.

Mama Liu did not say a word. Her mouth tightened, and she squeezed Petal's hand.

I couldn't stand around and listen to this. I had a job to do. "You are wrong, Empress. It's time you learned a lesson. We won't allow you to cause pain anymore or to harm and capture other living creatures. You took away the freedom of the Slow Willow Town people, but we're not going to let you get away with it anymore!" By the time I had finished my little speech, my heart was pounding, but I still felt power surging through me. I was ready to take on the empress—birds or no birds.

Unfortunately, my words just seemed to anger the empress. She began to get taller, until she was towering above us. Enormous black wings billowed and stretched behind her, and when I tried to make out her face, I couldn't, because it was shimmering and shifting before my eyes—half human one minute, multieyed and buglike the next. I shuddered and felt my bravery slip away from me. I noticed that the others looked just as scared as I suddenly felt.

"Good going, Hay Lin," Irma snapped.

"Always a good idea to tick off the bug queen."

I looked at her and shrugged my shoulders, as if to say, Can't do anything about it now! Clearly, the empress was angry.

"I will not be defied," she roared. Enraged, she grew even taller. From under her black wings, a swarm of scorpions shot out in the shape of an arrow. They headed straight for Mama Liu.

"No!" I screamed. Mama Liu didn't deserve to be hurt again. I flung out my hands and called on the winds. A gust of hot air began spinning, cyclonelike, through the room. Moving faster and faster, it collided with the scorpions, scattering them. But it wasn't finished. It kept blowing, breaking up the buggy pillars and curtains, catching all the little black bodies and hurling them around. The wind kept spinning until huge chunks of the room broke apart, letting in the sunlight.

In my rage, I had unleashed a monstrous wind. I could do nothing but sit back and see what happened next.

Through the wind and flying bugs, I saw that Will had called the Heart of Candracar into her hand. I could see its gentle light and feel the power it gave me, and I knew then that the others were helping, feeding me their strength through the Heart. My anger subsided and was replaced by an overwhelming feeling of love and pride in my friends. I couldn't have faced such evil without them.

The empress shrieked in fury as my winds continued to attack her and now began tearing at her wings. Then, just as the giant spider had done, she began to come apart. Before our very eyes, she became formless and vague. Her wings disintegrated completely, and within seconds, the rest of her blew apart. She had been no more solid than the spider.

"Wow," said Irma in an awed voice. "Now that's what I call finishing things off! Way to go, Hay Lin! You showed her."

The wind faded to a light breeze, and my knees buckled. I sat down on the hard marble floor, feeling completely drained. Turning to look around the damage, I felt my heart stop. Next to me lay the crumpled form of Mama Liu.

"No!" I screamed.

I fumbled for her wrist to see if I could feel a pulse. This couldn't be happening, I thought. What had I done? Had the scorpions gotten to her before I got to them? I had done everything I could do to protect her, and still, she had fallen. I wanted to weep.

"Grandmother!" Petal's voice was filled with the same anguish I felt. She flung herself down beside the woman. "Grandmother, please! Please be okay."

I held back a sob. Beneath my searching fingers, I could feel a small, fluttering pulse. But it was beating weakly, as if each tiny pulse might be the last.

We had to help her . . . immediately.

Before I could do anything, Mama Liu stirred. With a huge effort, she tried to sit up. "Petal, child, where are you? Let me feel your face. I had hoped that I could see it one more time."

"You mean you still can't see?" I asked in a gentle whisper. I didn't want to startle Mama Liu after all she'd been through, but I was worried and disappointed. I didn't want things to end like this for her.

"I see only the blackness," she replied sadly.

I felt myself swell up with anger. It was so unfair. To have come this far, to have fought this hard . . . for nothing! Mama Liu had been so brave when she faced up to a feared and cruel enemy. And she had done it without the magic that we had. She *deserved* to get her sight back. I had been sure that once the empress was destroyed, the curse would be lifted and Mama Liu's eyesight would be restored. I hated to think I had been wrong.

"Can anyone do anything to heal her eyes?" I asked, looking hopefully at my friends, who had gathered around us. They all had glum expressions on their faces as they shrugged their shoulders and shook their heads. I felt my eyes begin to well up with tears.

Will shook her head sympathetically. "I don't think so," she said, looking helpless and miserable. "I wish I could, but I just don't know how. I don't even know if the Heart could help at this point."

Cornelia silently shook her head, agreeing with Will.

"Sorry," Irma said, looking away.

Taranee sniffed. "It's not fair," she said, echoing my own thought. "Couldn't we ask the Oracle for help?"

I was about to answer her when I realized there were no longer just five of us in the circle. A sixth person had joined us.

It was my grandmother.

Somehow, in the midst of the chaos, she had slipped in, unnoticed by any of us.

I couldn't physically see her, but I knew she

was there. When I heard her voice I was certain.

"Liu . . . Liu, I need you to look at me." My grandmother's voice was gentle but persistent. Hearing it, I instantly felt calmer.

At the sound of Grandma's voice, Mama Liu straightened. "You came back!" she said, smiling.

"I told you I would," replied my grandmother. "I would not break my word."

"And I—I can see you!" Mama Liu exclaimed, reaching out in front of her.

I tried to make out what it was that Mama Liu was seeing, but although I *knew* my grandmother was there, she was still invisible to me. I felt my heart tighten and a familiar sadness grip my soul.

"I'm here, Little One. I'll always be here," Grandma said softly in my ear. "You have to have faith in me . . . and yourself." I smiled. Somehow I knew that no one else could hear that last caressing whisper but me. "Now, go and finish this mission. Find the empress."

And with that warning, she was gone.

Find the empress? What was Grandma talking about? She . . . she had come apart. I had destroyed her, hadn't I?

My thoughts were interrupted by a shriek of joy.

"I can see you," Mama Liu said. Her eyes

were locked on Petal's face, and they glistened with unshed tears. Her voice shook as she reached a hand out and said, "I can see you again!"

Their happiness was contagious. I smiled, forgetting for a moment that I still had work to do. But then I remembered Grandma's words and knew we had a task to finish.

I looked at my four friends. "We have to find the empress," I said, trying to sound as though I knew what I was talking about.

"What do you mean?" said Irma. "We just found her, remember? You scattered her all over the place! She's gone; let it go, Hay Lin!"

I shook my head stubbornly. "There must be some part of her remaining."

"But, Hay Lin, you saw for yourself," protested Will. "The empress came apart totally. There's nothing left of her except maybe a few bugs. What could possibly be left to find?"

I knew I sounded crazy, but I had to trust my grandmother. I looked at Will. "That might be true. But she came back before," I said. "It took her a long time, but she was able to gather herself together again. I don't want to take that chance. She needs to be completely destroyed."

"Well, fine, then. But where did she go?"

Cornelia asked. "What are we looking for?"

"Maybe we can try scrying to find her," Taranee suggested, shrugging her shoulders. "Ask our elements where she's gone."

Everyone nodded in agreement. It seemed like our only hope of finding the empress. Taranee lit a small flame and cradled it in her hand, staring into the flame. Cornelia put her palm flat against the ground, and Will clutched the Heart. Irma made herself a small pool on the floor of the throne room and gazed at its mirror-blank surface. And I closed my eyes and listened to the wind.

It only took a moment for the empress to be revealed. Opening my eyes, I could tell the others had found her, too.

"Let's get her!" cried Will, jumping up and raising her fist in the air.

We began running around the room, chasing something that was almost invisible. Finally, Irma threw herself to the floor, bringing both hands together.

"Gotcha!" she cried triumphantly. She stood up, hanging on to her catch. When we all drew nearer, we saw exactly what our scrying had shown us—one black beetle, slightly larger than the others, with a small white crown on its head.

"Petal, can you get me a jar?" asked Irma with a laugh. "One with a very good lid on it—we wouldn't want Her Majesty to leave her new home anytime soon!"

9

"Do you have to leave?" Petal asked, placing a small tray filled with food on the low table in front of us. The table was already groaning under the weight of all the food placed there earlier. "There's been so much to do here, we've hardly had time to honor you properly!"

"You've done far too much already," I replied. Then I patted my stomach and eyed the food. "I'm not sure we can handle much more honoring," I added with a smile.

It was several days after we had destroyed the empress, and we had spent the time making sure the people of Slow Willow Town were going to recover fully. We had also spent that time being honored. This consisted mostly of sitting still and smiling a lot while people offered compliments and everyone felt uncomfortable. There was also lots of eating! I hated to admit it, but I liked the Slow Willow Town people much better when they simply talked and acted as if we were ordinary human beings—not some kind of superheroes who would be offended if the townsfolk didn't bow low enough.

Mama Liu looked over at me, a smile twinkling in her lively black eyes as she addressed Petal. "Perhaps our guests would rather just have some tea, dear child. We embarrass them with our compliments, I think," she said wisely.

"But they deserve honor!" Petal protested, breaking into my thoughts.

"Indeed they do. But they know they are honored where it matters—in our hearts."

"Thank you, Mama Liu," I said, blushing at the praise. I sipped my tea. And from out of nowhere came the thought that now, at last, I had paid for my mirror. True, it wasn't a literal payment, but I had kept my grandmother's promise, and in return I had been rewarded with her closeness, her warmth, and her pride in me.

Still, I wasn't ready to go quite yet. I had one more thing to give to Mama Liu. From my pocket, where I had put it what seemed like ages ago, I pulled out the picture of my grandmother. It was slightly wrinkled from the wear and tear of doing battle, but the image was still clear.

"Mama Liu, I thought you should have this. Petal drew it . . . and it was why I followed her here," I said softly. "Without her talent I never would have known what was going on here. I know you will be proud to see what a great artist she is." Smiling, I placed the picture in Mama Liu's warm hand. True, at that moment I wished that I could have been giving my own grandmother a picture I had made . . . but this felt right.

"Thank you, Hay Lin," replied Mama Liu kindly. "This means the world to me. You have given me much today."

Without another word, she wrapped me in her arms and gave me a hug. I breathed in and, for a moment, felt like it was my grandmother's arms around me. I had never been prouder to be a member of W.I.T.C.H.

Soon after, we left Slow Willow Town. We trudged up the White Wind Mountain, back to the area where we had first met Petal. The wind chimes still swung gently in the breeze, making their tinkling music. It hadn't occurred to me that we would have any problem getting back until Irma piped up.

"It's not there," said Irma, looking around. "There's no mirror doorway!"

She was right. There was no trace of the oval mirror that had allowed us to get there. I felt a pit begin to grow in my stomach. This was bad news.

"Oh, that's just great," Cornelia scoffed. "Why is it that magic always manages to suck you in to things without any trouble, but then always has a problem getting you out afterward? It's some cruel joke—or a test—isn't it?"

"It's gotta come back," I said. "The Oracle would never leave us stranded here. We did our job, and now it's time to go back."

"We don't even need the mirror, guys," said Will, interrupting us before our conversation escalated into an argument. "We just have to use the Heart of Candracar to ask the Oracle to bring us home again. Plus, we have to go to Candracar anyway. We have a delivery to make." She pointed at the sealed jar I was carrying. Inside it, a very disgruntled-looking beetle kept butting its head against the glass.

I let out an "ahh" of understanding, and Cornelia sheepishly looked at the ground. Leave it to Will to point out the obvious answer.

Without another word, Will brought the Heart out, and we each placed our hands on the glowing orb, one on top of the other. The familiar warmth of the Heart ran through me.

Soon, the tinkling melody of Petal's wind chimes faded, and the mountainside around us disappeared.

"Welcome, Guardians." Once again, the Oracle welcomed us with his standard greeting.

We were in the pillared hall of the Temple of Candracar, surrounded by infinity. In the middle of the hall, the Oracle waited, smiling in welcome. While I was used to seeing him there, this time I looked around hoping to see someone else, too. I wasn't disappointed.

"Hello, Little One. And thank you for completing your mission." It was my grandmother's voice, full of love and pride. For a moment, I wanted to stay with her forever in Candracar—even if it meant leaving my old life behind.

That cannot be, the Oracle said silently, breaking in and reading my thoughts. *Your grandmother belongs here in Candracar. This is her home. Someday, you too may earn a place. But, for now, you must return to Heatherfield—your home.*

I knew that the Oracle was right. I felt tears in my eyes.

"I don't want to leave you," I whispered, throwing my arms around my grandmother's thin and familiar neck. I clung to her tightly. I didn't want to let go. "Please don't make me!"

"I know, Little One. But we shall see each other again. And your parents will miss you if you don't get back soon. Besides," she said, holding up an admonishing forefinger, "it's already *long* past your bedtime, young lady!"

She sounded so much like herself that I couldn't help giggling. Turning toward the Oracle, I held out the jar.

"Can you take care of Her Majesty?" I asked, nodding at the bug.

"I will. You have done the right thing in bringing her to me. Now her freedom can be limited until she has learned not to wield her power over others," the Oracle said aloud.

"Well, we did tell her we were going to teach her a lesson," Irma joked. "And it looks like this lesson could take a *very* long time."

A smile touched the Oracle's mouth.

"You may be right, Guardian," he said.

And then, time and space whirled around us, and once again we were back in Heatherfield.

The night was nearly over.

"I've got to get home," said Taranee once we had all transformed back into our non-Guardian selves. "My mother will be so angry if she finds out that I've been out all night."

"I think we should all be getting back," said

Will. "None of our parents would be happy if they knew what we had been up to."

The rest of the girls left. Before I turned to go, I looked into the cherry-tree branches above my head where the mirror and the lantern still swung gently. The lantern was no longer lit, and the mirror looked like an ordinary mirror. I knew that it would no longer take me back to the Valley of the Slow Willow River. It had served its purpose, and the magic had now left it. Gently, I untied the mirror, then lifted down the lantern as well. Liu's lantern. Well, at least now I knew why my grandmother had called it that.

I snuck quietly back into my house and fell into bed, the lamp and the mirror safely put away. I had barely gotten under the covers and drifted off, however, when I felt my mother's hand on my shoulder, shaking me awake.

"Wake up, Little One, wake up. There's been a message from the hospital. We must go there at once."

I sat up quickly. "Is Uncle Kao worse?" I asked, trying to keep the fear out of my voice.

"I don't know. They just called and said to come at once," my mother replied.

We drove to the hospital quickly, but once we got

there, everything seemed to slow down. I think we were all afraid of what we might find when we got to Uncle Kao's room.

What we found was a smiling Uncle Kao, sitting up in bed, carefully sipping from the cup of green tea that Lee was holding for him.

"I see you're feeling better," said my father, sitting down rather suddenly in a nearby visitor's chair.

The old man nodded. "Mmmm. Someone told me I wasn't going anywhere, so I might as well get on with life and stop scaring everybody."

My mouth dropped open. I knew exactly who had said those words.

I laughed. "I bet I know who told you that," I said, smiling.

Uncle Kao looked at me, his eyes oddly bright in his lined old face. Then he also smiled. "Perhaps you do, girl-child. Perhaps you do."

Reaching out, I put my hand on top of his. I felt a familiar swoosh of warmth and knew my grandmother was there, proudly watching over me—just as she always would.